THE
NIGHT BEFORE
CHRISTMAS
AND OTHER
HOLIDAY TALES

THE NIGHT BEFORE CHRISTMAS
AND OTHER
HOLIDAY TALES

Modern Publishing
A Division of Kappa Books Publishers, LLC.

Contents

The Night Before Christmas

Clement C. Moore

'Twas the night before Christmas,
    when all through the house

Not a creature was stirring,
    not even a mouse;

The stockings were hung
    by the chimney with care,

In hopes that St. Nicholas
    soon would be there.

The children were nestled
all snug in their beds,

While visions of sugar plums
danced in their heads.

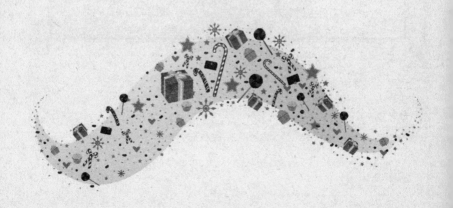

And Mama in her kerchief,
and I in my cap,

Had just settled our brains
for a long winter's nap,

When out on the lawn there
arose such a clatter,

I sprang from my bed to see
    what was the matter.

Away to the window
    I flew like a flash,

Tore open the shutters
    and threw up the sash.

The moon on the breast
of the new fallen snow

Gave the luster of midday
to objects below;

When what to my wondering
eyes should appear,

But a miniature sleigh
and eight tiny reindeer,

With a little old driver,
so lively and quick,

I knew in a moment
it must be St. Nick.

More rapid than eagles
his coursers they came,

And he whistled and shouted,
and called them by name:

"Now, Dasher! Now, Dancer!
Now, Prancer and Vixen!

On, Comet! On, Cupid!
On, Donder and Blitzen!

To the top of the porch,
to the top of the wall!

Now dash away, dash away,
dash away, all!"

As dry leaves before
   the wild hurricane fly,

When they meet with an obstacle,
   mount to the sky,

So up to the housetop
   the coursers they flew,

With the sleigh full of toys,
   and St. Nicholas, too.

And then in a twinkling
I heard on the roof

The prancing and pawing
of each little hoof.

As I drew in my head,
and was turning around,

Down the chimney St. Nicholas
came with a bound.

He was dressed all in fur,
    from his head to his foot,

And his clothes were all tarnished
    with ashes and soot.

A bundle of toys
    he had flung on his back,

And he looked like a peddler
    just opening his pack.

His eyes—how they twinkled,
    his dimples, how merry!

His cheeks were like roses,
    his nose like a cherry!

His droll little mouth
    was drawn up like a bow,

And the beard of his chin
    was as white as the snow;

The stump of a pipe
    he held tight in his teeth,

And the smoke it encircled
    his head like a wreath;

He had a broad face
    and a little round belly,

That shook when he laughed,
    like a bowlful of jelly.

He was chubby and plump,
  a right jolly old elf,

And I laughed when I saw him,
  in spite of myself;

A wink of his eye and
  a twist of his head,

Soon gave me to know
  I had nothing to dread.

He spoke not a word,
    but went straight to his work,

And filled all the stockings;
    then turned with a jerk,

And laying his finger aside
of his nose,

And giving a nod, up the
chimney he rose;

He sprang to his sleigh,
    to his team gave a whistle,

And away they all flew
    like the down of a thistle.

But I heard him exclaim,
  ere he drove out of sight,

"Happy Christmas to all,
  and to all a good night."

The Elves and the Shoemaker

There was once a shoemaker who, through no fault of his own, had become very poor.

"I am sorry to say, my dear," he said to his wife, "but all I have left in the shop is enough leather to make one pair of shoes."

In the evening, he cut out the leather for the shoes, planning to work on them the next day. Then he and his wife went to bed and fell asleep.

The next morning, the shoemaker went into his workshop, and was very surprised to find a completely finished pair of shoes sitting on the table.

"How did this happen?" he asked his wife in amazement.

"Why, I have no idea," she replied.

He picked up the shoes and examined them carefully.

"Not a stitch is out of place!" he exclaimed.

The shoes looked as though a master craftsman made them.

Later that day, a customer came in to the shoemaker's little shop.

"What a fine pair of shoes these are," the customer said, and he looked at the new pair of shoes.

He was so impressed with the finely crafted shoes that he paid more than the usual price for them.

The shoemaker used the money to buy enough leather to make two pairs of shoes. He cut out the leather that evening.

"I will start work on the new shoes first thing in the morning," he said to himself as he headed off to bed.

But when the shoemaker went into his shop in the morning, there was no need to do any work. Both pairs of shoes were already finished, although the shoemaker had no idea how. It was not long before customers bought the beautiful shoes. They paid such good prices that the shoemaker was able to buy enough leather for four more pairs of shoes.

The next morning, the shoemaker once again entered his workshop to find that the leather he had laid out the night before had been magically transformed into four pairs of finished shoes by morning! Very soon, the shoemaker was making a good living again and in to time at all, he became a wealthy man.

One evening just before Christmas, after the shoemaker had cut his leather, he said to his wife, "Let's stay up tonight and find out who has been helping us by making all of those beautiful shoes every night."

"What a wonderful idea," she said.

So they lit a candle and hid behind some clothes that were hanging in the corner, and waited.

At midnight, two little men wearing ragged and ripped clothes came in and began to work at the shoemaker's table. They picked up the leather with their tiny fingers.

The little men began to stitch and sew and hammer so skillfully and quickly, the shoemaker and his wife could not believe their eyes. The little men worked without stopping until all of the shoes lay finished on the table. Then they rushed away.

In the morning, the shoemaker's wife said, "Those little men have made us rich. How can we ever find a way to thank them?"

"They must be freezing running around in such tattered and threadbare clothes," said the shoemaker. "We could make them new outfits."

"What a fine idea," agreed his wife. "I'll make them each a coat, a vest and a pair of pants. And I'll knit them each a pair of stockings."

"And I shall make two fine pairs of little shoes," added the shoemaker.

That evening when everything was completed, they put their presents on the table in place of the cut-out leather.

"Let's stay up late and hide once more to see what the little men will do," said the shoemaker to his wife.

"I was just about to suggest the same thing!" she said.

At midnight the little men entered the shoemaker's workshop. They were ready to begin their nightly work. At first they were very surprised to see the new little clothes laid out for them instead of the leather. They were very soon filled with joy.

The two little men quickly put on their brand new clothes. They began to sing a very happy little tune.

"Now we are boys so pretty and neat, no longer will we cobble for others' feet!" they sang out with joy.

The little men were so excited about their new clothes that they skipped all around the room. They jumped over chairs and hopped onto benches. Finally they danced right out of the door and disappeared into the night.

The little men never came back to the shoemaker's workshop again. But, thanks to their help, the shoemaker prospered for as long as he lived and was very successful in everything he did.

The Twelve Days of Christmas

On the first day of Christmas,
My true love gave to me
A partridge in a pear tree.

On the second day of Christmas,
My true love gave to me
Two turtledoves
And a partridge in a pear tree.

On the third day of Christmas,
My true love gave to me
Three French hens,
Two turtledoves
And a partridge in a pear tree.

On the fourth day of Christmas,
My true love gave to me
Four calling birds,
Three French hens,
Two turtledoves
And a partridge in a pear tree.

On the fifth day of Christmas,
My true love gave to me
Five gold rings;
Four calling birds,
Three French hens,
Two turtledoves
And a partridge in a pear tree.

On the sixth day of Christmas,
My true love gave to me
Six geese a-laying,
Five gold rings;
Four calling birds,
Three French hens,
Two turtledoves
And a partridge in a pear tree.

On the seventh day of Christmas,
My true love gave to me
Seven swans a-swimming,
Six geese a-laying,
Five gold rings;
Four calling birds,
Three French hens,
Two turtledoves
And a partridge in a pear tree.

On the eighth day of Christmas,
My true love gave to me
Eight maids a-milking,
Seven swans a-swimming,
Six geese a-laying,

Five gold rings;
Four calling birds,
Three French hens,
Two turtledoves
And a partridge in a pear tree.

On the ninth day of Christmas,
My true love gave to me
Nine ladies dancing,
Eight maids a-milking,
Seven swans a-swimming,
Six geese a-laying,
Five gold rings;
Four calling birds,
Three French hens,
Two turtledoves
And a partridge in a pear tree.

On the tenth day of Christmas,
My true love gave to me
Ten lords a-leaping,
Nine ladies dancing,
Eight maids a-milking,
Seven swans a-swimming,
Six geese a-laying,
Five gold rings;
Four calling birds,
Three French hens,
Two turtledoves
And a partridge in a pear tree.

On the eleventh day of Christmas,
My true love gave to me
Eleven pipers piping,
Ten lords a-leaping,
Nine ladies dancing,
Eight maids a-milking,
Seven swans a-swimming,
Six geese a-laying,
Five gold rings;
Four calling birds,
Three French hens,
Two turtledoves
And a partridge in a pear tree.

On the twelfth day of Christmas,
My true love gave to me
Twelve drummers drumming,

Eleven pipers piping,
Ten lords a-leaping,

Nine ladies dancing,
Eight maids a-milking,
Seven swans a-swimming,
Six geese a-laying,

Five gold rings;
Four calling birds,
Three French hens,
Two turtledoves

And a partridge in a pear tree.

The Gift of the Magi

O. Henry

One dollar and eighty-seven cents was all that Della had. She counted it three times to make sure. That was all the money she had and tomorrow would be Christmas.

Della finished her cry. She stood by the window and looked out dully at a gray cat walking a gray fence in a gray backyard. Tomorrow would be Christmas Day, and she had only $1.87 with which to buy Jim a present. She had been saving every penny she could for months, with this result. Twenty dollars a week doesn't go far. Expenses had been greater than she had calculated. They always are. Only $1.87 to buy a present for Jim. Her Jim. Many a happy hour she had spent planning for something nice for him. Something fine and rare and sterling—something just a little bit near to being worthy of the honor of being owned by Jim.

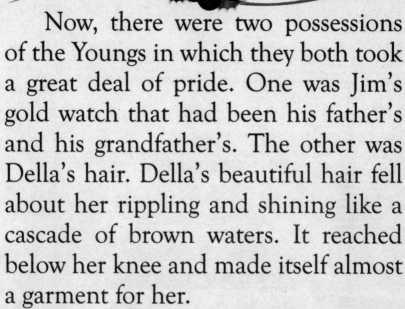

Now, there were two possessions of the Youngs in which they both took a great deal of pride. One was Jim's gold watch that had been his father's and his grandfather's. The other was Della's hair. Della's beautiful hair fell about her rippling and shining like a cascade of brown waters. It reached below her knee and made itself almost a garment for her.

Della put on her old brown jacket and her old brown hat. She scurried out the door and down the stairs to the street.

Where she stopped the sign read: "Mrs. Sofronie. Hair Goods of All Kinds." One flight up Della ran, and collected herself, panting.

"Will you buy my hair?"
asked Della.
"I buy hair," said Madame.
"Take your hat off and let's
have a look at it."
Down rippled the brown cascade.
"Twenty dollars," said Madame,
lifting the mass with
a practiced hand.
"Give it to me quick," said Della.

Della collected her twenty dollars and spent the next few hours ransacking the stores in search of the perfect gift for Jim.

She found it at last. It surely had been made for Jim and no one else. There was no other like it in any of the stores, and she had turned all of them inside out. It was a platinum fob chain simple and chaste in design. It would be perfect for Jim to hang his precious watch on. It cost Della twenty-one dollars, almost all of the money she had.

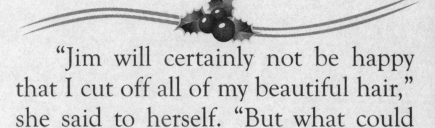

"Jim will certainly not be happy that I cut off all of my beautiful hair," she said to herself. "But what could I have done with only a dollar and eighty-seven cents?"

Before long, Della heard Jim's footsteps on the stairs. She hoped and prayed that Jim would still think she was pretty, even with such short hair.

The door opened and Jim stepped in and closed it. He looked thin and very serious. Poor fellow, he needed a new overcoat and he was without gloves. Jim stopped inside the door. His eyes were fixed upon Della, and there was an expression in them that she could not read, and it terrified her.

It was not anger, nor surprise, nor disapproval, nor horror, nor any of the sentiments that she had been prepared for. He simply stared at her fixedly with that peculiar expression on his face.

"Jim, darling," Della cried, "don't look at me that way. I had my hair cut off and sold because I couldn't have lived through Christmas without giving you a present. It'll grow out again—you won't mind, will you? I just had to do it. My hair grows awfully fast. Say 'Merry Christmas!' Jim, and let's be happy. You don't know what a beautiful, nice gift I've got for you."

"You've cut off your hair?" asked Jim.

"Cut it off and sold it," said Della.

"Don't you like me just as well, anyhow? I'm still me without my hair, aren't I?"

Jim looked about the room curiously.

"You say your hair is gone?" he said, with an air almost of idiocy.

Out of his trance Jim seemed quickly to wake. He hugged his Della.

Jim drew a package from his overcoat pocket and threw it upon the table.

"Don't make any mistake, Dell," he said, "about me. I don't think there's anything in the way of a haircut or a shave or a shampoo that could make me like my girl any less."

"But if you'll unwrap that package you will see why you had me going a while at first.

Della unwrapped the package with a quickness and suddenly started to cry. Her sobs were uncontrollable.

For there lay The Combs—the set of combs that Della had worshipped long in a store window. Beautiful combs, pure tortoise shell, with jeweled rims—that were just the shade to wear in the beautiful vanished hair.

They were expensive combs, she knew, and her heart had simply craved and yearned over them without the least hope of possession.

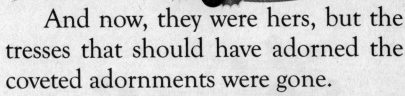

And now, they were hers, but the tresses that should have adorned the coveted adornments were gone.

But she hugged them to her bosom, and at length she was able to look up with dim eyes and a smile and say, "My hair grows so fast, Jim!"

And then Della leaped up like a little cat and cried, "Oh, oh!"

Jim had not yet seen his beautiful present. She held it out to him eagerly upon her open palm. The dull precious metal seemed to flash with a reflection of her bright and ardent spirit.

"Isn't it a dandy, Jim? I hunted all over town to find it. You'll have to look at the time a hundred times a day now. Give me your watch."

"I want to see how it looks on it."

Instead of obeying, Jim tumbled down on the couch and put his hands under the back of his head and smiled.

"Dell," said he, "I sold the watch to get the money to buy your combs."

The magi were wise men who brought gifts to the babe in the manger. They invented the art of giving Christmas presents. Being wise, their gifts were no doubt wise ones. Jim and Della most unwisely sacrificed for each other the greatest treasures of their house. But let it be said that of all who give gifts these two were the wisest.

They are the magi.

The Friendly Beasts

Jesus, our brother, kind and good,
Was humbly born in a stable rude.

And the friendly beasts around Him stood,
Jesus, our brother, kind and good.

"I," said the donkey,
shaggy and brown,
"I carried His mother
uphill and down;
I carried her safely
to Bethlehem town.
I," said the donkey,
shaggy and brown.

"I," said the cow,
all white and red,
"I gave Him my
manger for His bed;

I gave Him my hat
to pillow His head.
I," said the cow,
all white and red.

"I," said the dove from
the rafters high,
"I cooed Him to sleep so
He would not cry;
We cooed Him to sleep,
my mate and I.
I," said the dove
from the rafters high.

"I," said the sheep with
the curly horn,
"I gave Him my wool
for a blanket warm;

He wore my coat
on Christmas morn.
I," said the sheep
with the curly horn.

"I," said the rooster
with the shining eye,
"I crowed the news up
to the sky;
When the sun arose,
I crowed to the sky.
I," said the rooster
with the shining eye.

"I," said the camel,
all yellow and black,
"Over the desert
upon my back,
I brought Him a gift
in the Wise Men's pack.
I," said the camel,
all yellow and black.

So, every beast,
by some good spell,
In the stable dark was
glad to tell
Of the gift he gave Emmanuel.
The gift he gave Emmanuel.

The Fir Tree

Hans Christian Andersen

In a far corner of the forest, where plenty of warm sunshine and fresh air made a perfect home, grew a beautiful little fir tree. Even though the tree had a perfect home, it was not happy. It wanted very much to be big and tall, like the other trees that grew around it.

So discontented was the tree, that it took no pleasure in the sunshine, the birds, or the fluffy clouds that floated over it.

The tree grew each year. But no matter how much it grew it always complained that it was not quite big enough.

There was nothing else in the world that the tree cared about.

In the autumn the woodcutters came and cut down several of the tallest trees. The young fir, which was now grown to its full height, shuddered as the noble trees fell to the earth with a crash.

Then they were piled on top of each other, upon wagons, and drawn by horses out of the forest. "Where could they be going? What would become of them?" the young fir tree wondered.

He asked his friends, the swallows and storks.

They all had ideas, and, with every one, the fir tree wished even harder that he could share the fate of the larger trees.

But his friends told him to cherish and savor his youth, and not to waste it by wishing it away. He did not heed them. Christmas time drew near, and many young trees were cut down, some that were even smaller and younger than the fir tree.

These trees, which were chosen for their beauty, kept their branches, and were also laid on wagons, and taken far away out of the forest.

"Where are they going?" asked the fir tree. "They are not taller than I am?"

"We know, we know," sang the sparrows, "we have looked in the windows of the houses in the town. You would not believe what honor and glory they receive. They are dressed up in the most splendid manner. We have seen them standing in the middle of a warm room, and adorned with all sorts of beautiful things."

"I wonder whether anything so brilliant will ever happen to me," thought the fir tree.

"Rejoice in our friendship," said the air and the sunlight. "Enjoy your own bright life in the fresh air."

But the tree would not rejoice, though it grew taller every day and, winter and summer, its dark green foliage might be seen in the forests, while passersby would say, "What a beautiful tree!"

A short time before Christmas the discontented fir tree was the first to fall. As the axe cut sharply through the stem, the tree knew that it would never again see its dear old companions, the trees, nor the little bushes and flowers that had grown by its side.

The tree soon found itself being unpacked in the courtyard of a house, with several other trees. It heard a man say, "We only want one, and this is the prettiest. This is beautiful!"

Then came two servants who carried the fir tree into a large and beautiful apartment.

The fir tree trembled as it wondered what would become of it.

Then, it was adorned with the most beautiful trimmings. Once it was all decorated, children came running in to admire the tree.

"What are they doing? What will happen next?" thought the tree. The children rushed upon the tree and began to pull at its branches to remove the gifts that were hung upon the tree. There was such a riot that the branches cracked.

Then the children danced about with their pretty toys, and no one noticed the tree.

In the morning the servants came in. "Now," thought the fir tree, "all my splendor is going to begin again." But they dragged him out of the room and threw him on the floor, in a dark corner where no daylight shone, and there they left him.

"What does this mean?" thought the tree. "What am I to do here?"

Days and nights passed, and no one came near him. So the tree was completely hidden from sight as if it had never existed. He was so very lonely.

"Squeak, squeak," said a little mouse, creeping toward the tree. Then came another.

The mice asked the tree to tell them all about itself. The tree told of its old home in the forest and all about its youth. The mice thought that the tree must have had a very happy youth.

One morning people came to clear up the attic. The tree was dragged out. It once again was able to see bright sunlight. It thought that it must surely be beginning a new adventure.

The tree was placed next to a garden, amongst pretty flowers. The tree looked at its own branches, which were brittle and old. It had some old Christmas ornaments still stuck to it. One of the children remarked that it was now an ugly, old fir tree.

The tree was very sad. It wished that it had enjoyed its youthful days in the forest, instead of complaining and wishing for something else. But it was too late.

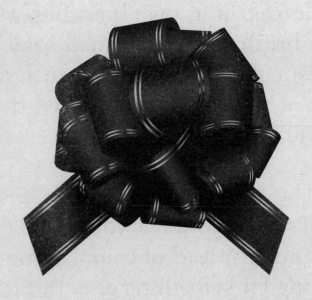

Christmas Carols

Deck the Halls

Deck the halls with boughs of holly,
Fa la la la la, la la la la!
'Tis the season to be jolly,
Fa la la la la, la la la la!
Don we now our gay apparel,
Fa la la, la la la, la la la!
Troll the ancient yuletide carol,
Fa la la la la, la la la la!

See the blazing yule before us,
Fa la la la la, la la la la!
Strike the harp and join the chorus,
Fa la la la la, la la la la!
Follow me in merry measure,
Fa la la, la la la, la la la!
While I tell of yuletide treasure,
Fa la la la la, la la la la!

Jingle Bells

Dashing through the snow
In a one-horse open sleigh
O'er the fields we go
Laughing all the way.
Bells on bob-tail ring
Making spirits bright
What fun it is to ride and sing
A sleighing song tonight.

Jingle bells, jingle bells
Jingle all the way,
Oh what fun it is to ride
In a one-horse open sleigh,
Oh, Jingle bells, jingle bells
Jingle all the way,
Oh what fun it is to ride
In a one-horse open sleigh.

A day or two ago
I thought I'd take a ride
And soon Miss Fanny Bright
Was seated by my side;
The horse was lean and lank
Misfortune seemed his lot,
We got into a drifted bank
And there we got upsot.

Jingle bells, jingle bells Jingle all the way,
Oh what fun it is to ride
In a one-horse open sleigh,
Oh, jingle bells, jingle bells
Jingle all the way,
Oh what fun it is to ride
In a one-horse open sleigh.

A day or two ago The story I must tell
I went out on the snow
And on my back I fell;
A gent was riding by
In a one-horse open sleigh
He laughed as there I sprawling lie
But quickly drove away.

Jingle bells, jingle bells Jingle all the way,
Oh what fun it is to ride
In a one-horse open sleigh,
Oh, jingle bells, jingle bells
Jingle all the way,
Oh what fun it is to ride
In a one-horse open sleigh.

Now the ground is white,
Go it while you're young,
Take the girls tonight
And sing this sleighing song.
 Just get a bob-tailed bay,
Two-forty for his speed,
Then hitch him to an open sleigh
And crack! You'll take the lead.

Jingle bells, jingle bells Jingle all the way,
Oh what fun it is to ride
In a one-horse open sleigh,
Oh, jingle bells, jingle bells
Jingle all the way,
Oh what fun it is to ride
In a one-horse open sleigh.

We Wish You a Merry Christmas

We wish you a Merry Christmas,
We wish you a Merry Christmas,
We wish you a Merry Christmas,
And a Happy New Year!

Good tidings we bring
To you and your kin;
We wish you a Merry Christmas
And a Happy New Year!

Now bring us some figgy pudding,
Now bring us some figgy pudding,
Now bring us some figgy pudding,
And bring some out here!

Good tidings we bring
To you and your kin;
We wish you a Merry Christmas
And a Happy New Year!

For we all like figgy pudding,
We all like figgy pudding,
We all like figgy pudding,
So bring some out here!

Good tidings we bring
To you and your kin;
We wish you a Merry Christmas
And a Happy New Year!

And we won't go until
we've got some,
We won't go until we've got some,
We won't go until we've got some,
So bring some out here!

Good tidings we bring
To you and your kin;
We wish you a Merry Christmas
And a Happy New Year!

Joy to the World

Joy to the world, the Lord is come!
Let earth receive her King;
Let every heart prepare Him room,
And heaven and nature sing,
And heaven and nature sing,
And heaven, and heaven,
and nature sing.

Joy to the world, the Savior reigns!
Let men their songs employ;
While fields and floods, rocks,
hills and plains
Repeat the sounding joy,
Repeat the sounding joy,
Repeat, repeat, the sounding joy.

No more let sins and sorrows grow,
Nor thorns infest the ground;
He comes to make
His blessings flow
Far as the curse is found,
Far as the curse is found,
Far as, far as, the curse is found.

He rules the world with
truth and grace,
And makes the nations prove
The glories of His righteousness,
And wonders of His love,
And wonders of His love,
And wonders, wonders, of His love.

Hark! The Herald Angels Sing

Hark! the herald angels sing,
"Glory to the new born King,
Peace on earth, and mercy mild,
 God and sinners reconciled!"
Joyful, all ye nations rise,
Join the triumph of the skies;
With th' angelic host proclaim,
"Christ is born in Bethlehem!"
 Hark! the herald angels sing,
"Glory to the new born King!"

179

Christ, by highest heaven adored;
Christ, the everlasting Lord;
Late in time behold him come,
Offspring of a virgin's womb.
Veiled in flesh the Godhead see;
Hail th' incarnate Deity,
Pleased as man with man to dwell,
Jesus, our Emmanuel.
Hark! the herald angels sing,
"Glory to the new born King!"

Hail the heaven-born
Prince of Peace!
Hail the Sun of Righteousness!
Light and life to all he brings,
Risen with healing in his wings.
Mild he lays his glory by,
Born that man no more may die,
Born to raise the sons of earth,
Born to give us second birth.
Hark! the herald angels sing,
"Glory to the new born King!"

Come, Desire of nations, come,
Fix in us thy humble home;
Rise, the woman's conquering Seed,
Bruise in us the serpent's head.
Adam's likeness, Lord, efface;
Stamp thine image in its place.
Second Adam from above,
Reinstate us in thy love.
Hark! the herald angels sing,
"Glory to the new born King!"

Adam's likeness, Lord, efface,
Stamp Thine image in its place:
Second Adam from above,
Reinstate us in Thy love.
Let us Thee, though lost, regain,
Thee, the Life, the inner man:
O, to all Thyself impart,
Formed in each believing heart.
Hark! the herald angels sing,
"Glory to the newborn King!"

It Came Upon a Midnight Clear

It came upon a midnight clear,
That glorious song of old,
From angels bending near the earth
To touch their harps of gold:
"Peace on the earth, good will to men,
From heav'n's all gracious King!"
The world in solemn stillness lay
To hear the angels sing.

Still thru the cloven skies they come
With peaceful wings unfurled,
And still their heav'nly music floats
O'er all the weary world:
Above its sad and lowly plains
They bend on hov'ring wing,
And ever o'er its Babel sounds
The blessed angels sing.

And ye, beneath life's crushing load,
Whose forms are bending low,
Who toil along the climbing way
With painful steps and slow,
Look now! for glad and golden hours
Come swiftly on the wing:
O rest beside the weary road
And hear the angels sing.

For lo, the days are hast'ning on,
By prophet bards foretold,
When with the ever circling years
Comes round the age of gold;
When peace shall over all the earth
Its ancient spendors fling,
And the whole world give back the song
Which now the angels sing.

Treasury of Illustrated Classics